Shelby Seagull and the Painted Shells

Written and illustrated
by Andy McGuinness

From the Whistle-On-Sea series

For Archie and Will

Come with me to Whistle-On-Sea...

There was a lovely smell of the sea in the air at Whistle-on-Sea. There was also a strong smell of paint.

Megan, Sam and a few of the gang were busy painting shells outside Beach Hut Betty.

They often spent mornings filling up Bertie Bucket with all sorts of different shaped shells they found on the beach ready to be painted in the afternoon.

Painting them was the fun part and everyone wanted to join in. Quite often Megan and Sam would have more helpers than they had paintbrushes.

Today, Willie Whelk and Larry Lobster were helping. Larry had never used a paintbrush before and it took some time for him to get the hang of holding it in his big claw.

"This is fun," he said cheerfully. "But I can't paint my shells as well as you can Willie."

"Yours are certainly very colourful," replied Willie. "They'll be great for decorating Beach Hut Betty."

"The more colourful they are, the better they are for selling too," said Sam full of encouragement

As well as using the shells to decorate Beach Hut Betty, Sam and Megan would sell them to people on the beach to help raise money for the Royal Navy Lifeboat Institute. They were the brave men and women who rescued people out at sea.

"What do you think?" said Willie holding up a shell for everyone to see.

"I've done stripes, splodges, and swirly patterns. What shall I paint now?"

"Paint me," said Suzy Starfish who was watching from the groynes with Marcel Moulé. "I'm a star!"

"That would be great, but there's just one problem," said Megan peering into an empty paint pot.

"We've run out of paint!"

"But we've still got lots of shells to paint," said Larry with paint all over him. "What are we going to do?"

Watching from the roof of Beach Hut Betty was Shelby Seagull. He had an idea.

"I've seen fishermen painting their boats in the boatyard. They often throw out old tins of paint. I'll see what they've got."
"Good thinking, Shelby," said Sam. "Do you need help to carry them?"

"No thanks, a beak and claws will do the trick!" replied Shelby and off he flew.

Shelby loved flying over Whistle-on-Sea on hot sunny days. He loved seeing all the boys and girls playing happily on the beach and in the sea.

"Boatyard ahoy!" he chuckled to himself sounding like a pirate.

He could see where all the old pots of paint had been piled up to be thrown away and swooped down.

'These will be great," he said pleased with his find. He grabbed a pot in each claw, one in his beak and took off.

They were heavier than he thought, but soon Shelby had Beach Hut Betty in his sight.

"Here's Shelby!" cried Bertie. "And he's got bucket loads of paint."

"Hurray!" cheered Willie.

"Okay gang, let's get the rest of these shells painted," said Megan.

"Come on Suzy," said Willie waving his brush. "Time to do your portrait."

Suzy posed for Willie, Larry painted more splodges and Megan and Sam worked their way through the rest of the shells.

As each shell was painted, Marcel and Shelby laid them out around the beach and on the groynes so they would dry in the sun.

Willie put the finishing touches to his portrait of Suzy and everyone gathered round to see.

"That's brilliant Willie, you're so clever," said Marcel. "We should be able to charge a bit extra for that shell."

"You're right. But it's too late to sell them now. It's starting to get dark," said Megan.

"Let's leave the shells to dry overnight and go for tea and cake in Beach Hut Betty."

As the shells were left drying, everyone tucked in to cups of tea and slices of delicious fruit cake.

"We've all earned this," said Larry, exhausted from the day's painting. "Now I'm feeling really tired," he yawned

"Me too," said Willie struggling to keep his eyes open.

In fact, everyone was feeling sleepy from the day's work and soon Megan, Sam, Larry, Willy, Bertie, Sandy and Shelby were fast asleep.

A little while later they were woken by a scurrying noise outside on the decking. Kelvin Crab burst through the door full of excitement.

"Wake up! Everyone, wake up!" he urged. "You should see the beach, it's all lit up for a party."

Megan lifted herself out of her deckchair and went to see what Kelvin was so excited about.

"Wow!" gasped Megan, as the others joined her outside in the dark.

"Bucket loads of glowing light," said Bertie amazed.

"Dig it!" cried Sandy Spade.

The beach was indeed all lit up with beautiful glowing colours. Not from lights, but from their painted shells.

"What is it?" asked Larry puzzled and also glowing with speckles of coloured paint.

"The paint Shelby found at the boatyard must have been luminous paint, which means it glows in the dark," explained Sam.

"Oh dear," said Shelby "Sorry, everyone."

"Don't be silly," said Kelvin. "It's the perfect light show for a rock concert."

Kelvin strapped on his guitar. "Come on Crabettes, let's rock!"

Suddenly the beach was filled with the sound of music as well as glowing light.

"Let's dance," said a luminous Larry to everyone.

And that's just what they did, between the moonlit sky and the shell-lit beach, until it was time for bed.

What fun!

The End

More stories in the Whistle-On-Sea series

Guitar-playing Kelvin Crab is planning to put on a rock concert at the Rock Pool, with his band the Crabettes. He decides to send a message in a bottle to tell all his friends. Realising few people will see it and not wanting Kelvin to be left feeling disappointed, Megan and the gang secretly plan other ways to draw the crowds. But will it work or will the evening be a disaster? Find out in Kelvin Crab and the Message in a Bottle.

Bertie Bucket and Sandy Spade are collecting shells to paint on the beach. They find an Oyster Shell, which they hope will contain a pearl. But when an evil seagull called Bagshot kidnaps Bertie and the Oyster Shell, it's left to Shelby Seagull to save the day. Find out how in Bertie Bucket and the Precious Pearl.

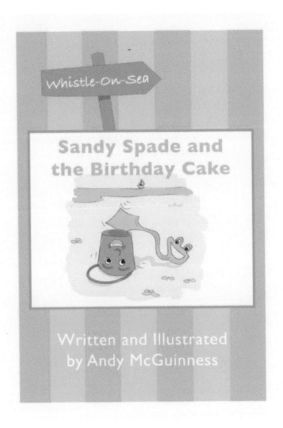

Whistle-On-Sea

Sandy Spade and
the Birthday Cake

Written and Illustrated
by Andy McGuinness

It's Megan's birthday, but Bertie Bucket and Sandy Spade don't have
the right ingredients to make her a birthday cake. To everyone's
excitement, Sandy suggests they make it from sand and so the
gang sets about making the best birthday cake ever. But when they
come to present it to Megan, they can't believe their eyes -
someone has started to eat it. Find out who in Sandy Spade and
the Birthday Cake.

Follow us on Facebook

ABOUT THE AUTHOR

Andy McGuinness has spent his career as an advertising copywriter in London. Inspired by many happy summers spent in Whitstable with his two small boys, he has written the Whistle-On-Sea series.

Printed in Poland
by Amazon Fulfillment
Poland Sp. z o.o., Wrocław

53071605R00016